This book belongs to

....

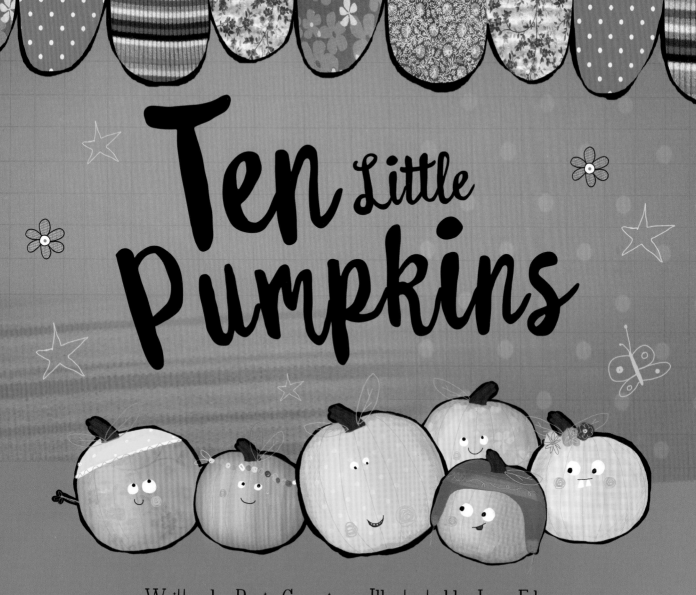

Ten Little Pumpkins

Written by Rosie Greening · Illustrated by Lara Ede

make
believe
ideas

10 little pumpkins
are growing in a line.

Then a **farmer** picks one up
and that **leaves** . . .

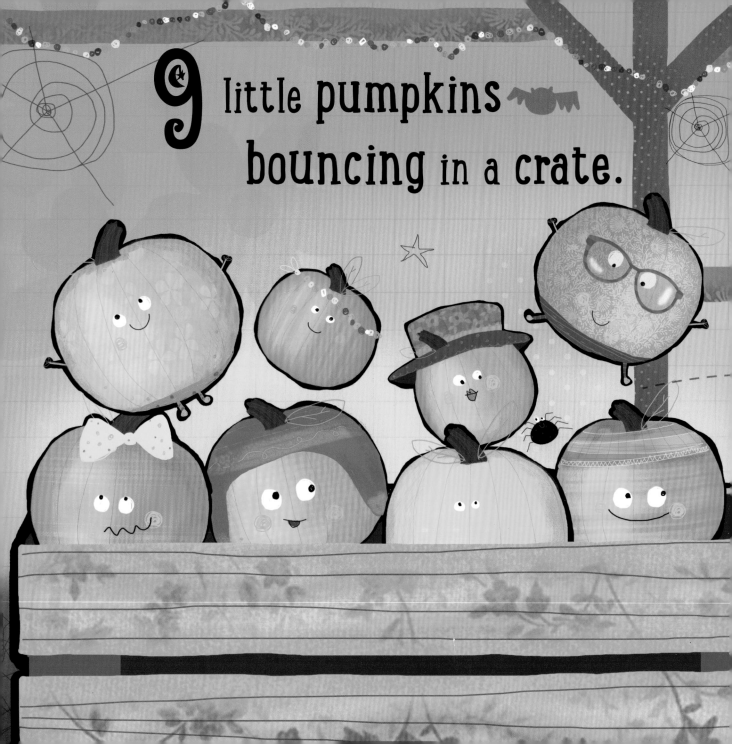

9 little pumpkins bouncing in a crate.

One decides to **bounce away**
and that leaves . . .

A pony **carries** one away

and that **leaves** . . .

7 little pumpkins doing **magic** tricks.

Eek!

Then one pumpkin disappears
and that leaves . . .

POOF!

6 little pumpkins
going for a drive.

TOWN

One jumps out to trick-or-treat
and that leaves . . .

4 little pumpkins
as happy as can be.

3 little pumpkins playing peekaboo.

Point to who you think is going to take him **off the shelf!**

Arrrr!

10 little pumpkins make such a **perfect** scene,

glowing all together on
the night of **Halloween!**

The End